THE MYSTERY AT THE FAIR

created by

GERTRUDE CHANDLER WARNER

Illustrated by Charles Tang

SCHOLASTIC INC.
New York Toronto London Auckland Sydney

Activities by Nancy E. Krulik

Activity illustrations by Alfred Giuliani

ISBN 0-590-56902-3

12 11 10 9 8 7 6 5 4 3 2 1   6 7 8 9/9 0 1/0

Printed in the U.S.A.   40

First Scholastic printing, March 1996

Contents

CHAPTER 1

Grandfather's Birthday Present

"Look at that!" Violet Alden said as she pointed to a beautiful book on the shelf of the Greenfield Bookshop. The shelf was high above her head. "I'll bet Grandfather would love to have that book for his birthday. I want to look at it more closely, but I can't reach it."

Jessie, who was twelve and a little taller than her ten-year-old sister, tried to take the book down for a closer look.

"I can't reach it either," Jessie said.

"Maybe Henry can," Violet suggested. "He's pretty tall for a fourteen-year-old."

"Henry, can you help us?" Jessie said. "I think Violet's found the perfect birthday gift for Grandfather."

"Where is it?" Henry asked.

"It's that book up there about the history of Greenfield," Violet said, pointing to the shelf. "You know how much Grandfather loves to collect old books. Will you get it down for us?"

"Sure," Henry said. He stretched as far as he could but the book was still out of reach.

"I can help," said Benny, their six-year-old brother.

"I'm afraid you're not tall enough yet," Jessie said, smiling down at her little brother.

"I'm tall enough if Henry picks me up," Benny said.

"That's a great idea," Violet said.

Henry picked up Benny. Benny grabbed the leather-bound book and handed it to Jessie.

"See," Benny said happily. "I told you I could help."

"Let me see the book, Jessie," Violet said. The children gathered around Violet as she turned page after page of the beautiful book.

"You're right, Violet," Henry said. "Out of all the things we've looked at in Greenfield, this is the perfect present."

"I know Grandfather will love this book," Jessie said. "He'll be so surprised."

Grandfather Alden's birthday was on Sunday, just a few days away. The children had been shopping all morning hoping to find the right gift for their wonderful grandfather.

"How much does it cost, Violet?" Henry asked.

"I'm not sure," Violet said. "There's no price tag on it."

"Let's ask Mr. Owens," Benny said. The children took the book to the counter. Mr. Owens, the owner of the Greenfield Bookshop, greeted them with a smile.

"Well, children," Mr. Owens said. "Have you finished your shopping?"

"Yes!" Benny said. "We want to buy *The History of Greenfield* for our grandfather. It's a birthday present."

Mr. Owens took the book and looked at it closely.

"That's the same book your grandfather was admiring the other day. He was in a hurry and said he'd be back to buy it later."

"Really?" Violet said. "Then we must buy it for him and surprise him."

"We couldn't find a price tag," Henry said. "Can you tell us how much it costs?"

"This book costs $50," Mr. Owens said.

"That's a lot of money," Benny said.

"Yes," Mr. Owens said. "But this book is leather and very old."

"It *is* beautiful," Jessie agreed. "But it costs more money than we have right now."

"Well," Mr. Owens said. "I can hold this book for you until Saturday. Maybe you'll have more money by then."

"That would be wonderful," Henry said. "I know we can think of a way to earn some extra money by then."

"I'm sure we can if we try hard enough," Jessie said.

"Thank you, Mr. Owens," Violet said. "We'll be back on Saturday."

The children left the bookshop and started to walk home. They tried to think of ways they could earn the money they needed to buy Grandfather's birthday present.

"Maybe I can cut grass or work in a garden the way I did when we lived in the boxcar," Henry said.

"That's a good idea, Henry," Jessie said.

After their parents died, the four Alden children lived in an old abandoned boxcar in the woods. They knew their grandfather was looking for them, but they thought he was mean. But when their grandfather found them, the children realized how kind he was. Now the Boxcar Children lived in their Grandfather's lovely old house in Greenfield. Mr. Alden had even moved their boxcar home into his backyard as a surprise.

"I'm hungry," Benny said. "I think better when my stomach is full."

"That's true," Violet said, laughing. "It is almost lunchtime."

"I'll race you to that lamppost in front of our house, Benny," Henry said. "The faster we run, the sooner you can eat lunch."

"Okay," Benny said. He raced down the street. His brother and sisters ran after him.

"I beat all of you," Benny said as he swung around the light pole in front of their house.

"Yes, you did," Violet said. "There's nothing like thinking about lunch to make you move quickly."

The children all laughed. Benny was always ready to eat.

"Look at this," Violet said, pointing to a sign on the lamppost.

COME ONE AND ALL TO THE
GREENFIELD COUNTY FAIR!
FRIDAY AND SATURDAY!
RIDES! RIDES! RIDES!
LIVESTOCK SHOW!
MARCHING BANDS!
GREAT EVENTS FOR ADULTS
AND CHILDREN!
$25 CASH PRIZES FOR THE BEST
ARTWORK
BAKED GOODS
CRAFTS
FILL OUT THE FORM BELOW

TO ENTER. ALL ENTRIES MUST
BE ACCOMPANIED BY AN
OFFICIAL FORM.

"Maybe we can make something to enter in the fair," Henry said. "If we win, we can use the money to buy Grandfather's birthday present."

"That's a wonderful idea," Jessie said.

Violet looked at the brightly colored poster and began to smile. "I know what I am going to do! I'll paint a picture."

"Mrs. McGregor helped Benny and me make a blueberry pie once," Henry said. "Maybe we could bake another one and enter it in the fair."

"That's a good idea," Jessie said. "The blueberries are ripe now. We could pick some this afternoon after lunch."

"Why don't we take a picnic lunch with us and go to the blueberry patch now," Violet said. "The sooner we get started the better."

"Maybe I can make something to enter in

the contest, too," Jessie said. "Surely one of us will win something."

Henry began tearing off entry blanks. One for Violet, one for Jessie, and one for himself and Benny.

A slender man, who was wearing a baseball cap, crossed the street and quickly approached the children.

"Hello," the man said. "Are you children going to use those forms or are you just playing around?"

"We're going to enter the fair competition," Henry said.

"We're hoping that we win so we can buy a birthday present for our grandfather," Jessie explained.

"Winning that money won't be easy," the man said. "I can tell you that for a fact."

"Well, we can try," Violet said. "As long as we try we have a chance of winning."

"Maybe," said the man. "If you're very, very lucky. What are your names and what kinds of projects were you going to enter?"

"Well," Jessie said a little uneasily, "my

name is Jessie Alden. I'm entering the crafts competition. This is my sister, Violet. She's entering some artwork." Why was this man asking so many questions?

"Henry and I are going to bake a blueberry pie," Benny said. "My name is Benny. What's yours?"

"I've got to go now," the man said quickly. "See you later." He crossed the street and hurried away.

"How mysterious," Jessie said. "I wonder why he was so interested in our fair projects?"

"Did you notice that he didn't answer when Benny asked him his name?" Henry said.

"Maybe he's a little shy," said Violet. She was also shy about meeting new people. "Or maybe he was just in a hurry."

"I'm in a hurry, too," Benny said as he tugged on Henry's arm. "I'm ready to eat lunch."

"So am I," Violet said. "Let's go inside."

CHAPTER 2

The Picnic

"Well, now," Mr. Alden said with a chuckle when the children entered the house. "My early birds have returned."

"We had a lot of things to do," Henry said.

"Are you going away on a business trip, Grandfather?" Violet said when she saw his garment bag.

"Yes," Mr. Alden said. "But only for a few days. I have a meeting to attend in New York."

"Will you be away on your birthday?" Henry asked.

"No," Mr. Alden said. "I'll be back by noon on Sunday. I'd almost forgotten that's my birthday."

"We didn't forget," Benny said.

Mr. Alden's eyes twinkled as he looked from one grandchild to the next. He knew they were up to something.

"Let's go eat lunch now," Jessie said quickly. She didn't want Benny to accidentally tell their Grandfather about the surprise party they were planning.

"Good idea," Violet said. "I think I smell cookies."

"Cookies!" Benny said. "See you later, Grandfather. Have a nice trip." He began to run down the hall that led to the kitchen.

"You children better hurry," Grandfather said, laughing. "Or there won't be anything left. Take care and I'll see you all Sunday afternoon."

The children said goodbye to their grandfather. Then they quickly ran down the hall after Benny. The delicious smell of freshly baked cookies greeted them as they entered the kitchen.

"There you are," Mrs. McGregor, the Alden's housekeeper, said with a smile. "I've just finished taking the last pan of chocolate chip cookies out of the oven."

"I love chocolate chip cookies," Benny said as he helped Mrs. McGregor remove the cookies from the pan. He picked one up, but before he could eat it, Jessie stopped him.

"You can have some cookies after you eat your lunch," Jessie said. "May we pack a picnic lunch, Mrs. McGregor? We're going to pick blueberries."

"Of course," Mrs. McGregor said. "It's a lovely day for a picnic. I've already made some sandwiches for you."

"Two sandwiches for me please," Benny said. "Let's pack some doggie biscuits for Watch, too. He'll want to come with us."

"Good idea," Mrs. McGregor said.

With everyone helping, it didn't take long to pack the picnic basket. Benny whistled for Watch, and the dog ran happily ahead of the children as they walked down the road to the woods. The older children took turns car-

rying the picnic basket. Benny carried the blueberry buckets.

"Let's sit under that tree," Jessie suggested. "It will be nice and cool there."

"I don't care where we eat as long as we eat soon," Benny said.

"Help me spread this blanket and then we'll eat," Henry said.

The two boys spread the blanket. Before they could unpack their lunch, the children heard a strange sound.

"What was that?" Jessie asked.

Watch leapt to his feet and began to bark. Then he ran into the woods. Henry chased after him.

"Wait, Henry," Jessie called out. "We'll all go with you."

"This reminds me of the time we heard that strange noise in the woods near our box-car," Violet said as they hurried after Henry.

"Violet! Jessie! Over here," Henry called.

They found Henry talking with a girl about Jessie's age. She was wearing a purple top and matching shorts. She looked very worried and there were tears in her eyes.

"This is Courtney Jenkins," Henry said. "Courtney, I want you to meet my sisters, Jessie and Violet, and my little brother, Benny."

"Hello," Courtney said softly. She wiped the tears away from her smooth brown cheeks and tried to smile.

"Hi," Benny said.

"Nice meeting you," Violet said.

"Hello, there," Jessie said. "What's wrong, Courtney?"

"My brother Michael is lost somewhere in these woods," Courtney said. "We moved into a house on Murray Street a few days ago. Today, we decided to do a little exploring. Michael wandered off while I was picking some flowers."

"Don't worry," Violet said. "We'll help you find him."

The children began searching for Michael. They'd only been looking for a short time when they heard Benny calling them.

"Here he is!" Benny said excitedly. "I found him!"

A small boy sat in the center of a large

patch of blueberries. His hands and mouth were full of the ripe fruit.

"Michael," Courtney said. "Why didn't you answer me? I've been calling you for more than an hour!"

The little boy slowly chewed and swallowed the mouthful of berries.

"I heard you, Courtney," Michael said. "But every time you called me my mouth was full. You told me don't ever talk with food in your mouth!"

The children all laughed. Courtney pulled her brother to his feet. She wiped a blue smudge off his small brown chin.

"I guess I can't be too mad at you," Courtney said. "These blueberries do look delicious."

"They sure do," Benny said, "but I'm just not hungry anymore."

"You're not?" cried Violet.

"No," Benny said. "Now I'm starving!"

CHAPTER 3

New Friends

Henry brought the picnic basket over to where Benny had found Michael. The girls spread the blanket near a tree. The Aldens shared their delicious lunch with Courtney and Michael.

"It's a good thing we packed some extra goodies for lunch," Jessie said as she watched Benny and Michael divide the last few chocolate chip cookies.

"This is the first time I've ever met anyone who loves to eat as much as Michael does," Courtney said, smiling.

"It looks like Benny's found a friend in more ways than one," Violet said.

After they finished eating, the children began to pick the blueberries.

"These blueberries are going to make a prize-winning pie for the county fair," Henry said.

"What fair?" Courtney asked.

"Every year, Greenfield has a county fair," Jessie explained. "This year they have a $25 cash prize for the best baked goods, the best art project, and the best craft project."

"Henry and I are going to bake a blueberry pie," Benny told Michael.

"I want to help," Michael said. "Blueberry pie with ice cream on top tastes good."

"This pie is for the fair contest, Michael," Henry said.

"That's okay," Michael said. "We can make two pies. One for the fair and one for us."

"That's a great idea," said Benny.

"Well, then," Jessie said. "If you're going to make two pies, you and Benny will have to stop eating the blueberries as fast as we put them in the bucket!"

"Let's have a blueberry picking race," Violet suggested.

"Yes," Henry said. "Let's see who fills their bucket first."

"Ready, set, go!" Courtney said.

The children began to pick the berries as fast as they could. Soon their buckets were filled with the sweet fruit.

"We won! We won!" Michael and Benny said, holding up their bucket.

"There's nothing like teamwork," Henry said. "Now we have plenty of blueberries to make into a pie!"

"Two pies!" Michael and Benny said together.

Everyone laughed.

"I think I'd like to enter something in the fair, too," Courtney said.

"We can show you where the entry forms are," Violet said. "The poster is on a lamppost near our house. Your new house on Murray Street is only three blocks away from where we live. You can walk home with us."

As they headed home, the girls tried to decide what they would make to enter in the fair.

"I love to make jewelry," Jessie said. "Maybe I can make something that will win a prize."

"I love making jewelry, too," Courtney said, smiling at her new friend.

"I think I'm going to paint a picture," Violet said.

"Let me guess," Henry said. "I'll bet you're going to paint a picture of some violets."

"Yes," Violet said, laughing. "But there will be some other pretty flowers in the picture, too."

The children continued to walk and talk until suddenly Henry stopped.

"Look!" Henry said, pointing to the lamppost where the entry forms had been. "Someone's torn up the poster!"

The children gathered around the post. Scraps of paper littered the ground.

"Who would do something like this?" Henry said as he picked up the bits of paper.

"I'll bet it was the man in the baseball cap," Benny said.

"What man?" Courtney asked.

"There was a man who was here earlier," Jessie explained. "He was asking us a lot of questions about our entries."

"But why would he tear up all the entry forms?" Michael asked. "That's mean."

"It's a mystery to me," Henry said. He looked at his sister and grinned.

"We love mysteries," Jessie explained to Courtney.

"Well, this looks like a good one," Courtney said. "I really want to enter that craft contest. I wonder where I can get another entry form?"

"We can make something together," Jessie suggested. "That way we can use the same form."

"Thank you," Courtney said. "If we work together it won't take very long to make something."

"And working together makes the project more fun," Jessie said. "Why don't you come over tomorrow morning so we can get started."

"That will be fine," Courtney said. "See you then."

"We can bake our pies tomorrow, too," Benny said.

"Yes," Michael said. "One for the contest and one to eat."

"I can hardly wait until tomorrow," Benny said as he waved good-bye to their new neighbors. "I love blueberry pie."

The next morning, Violet and Jessie got up early and went out to the boxcar. They had just opened the boxes that held their art supplies when they heard someone calling their names.

"Jessie! Violet!" Courtney called out. "Where are you?"

"We're in the boxcar," Violet said.

"Here we are, Courtney," Jessie said, waving to her new friend from the doorway. "Where's Michael?"

"He's in the kitchen with Henry and

Benny," Courtney replied. "Mrs. McGregor is showing them how to make pie crust."

"I can't wait to see how their pies turn out," Violet said.

"I can't wait to taste one," Jessie said.

"You're starting to sound like Michael and Benny," Courtney said as she climbed inside.

Jessie and Violet showed Courtney their boxcar treasures. Courtney smiled when she saw Benny's pink cup with the crack in it.

"This is a great place to play," Courtney said.

"It sure is," Jessie agreed. "We love it out here."

"You're just in time," Violet said. "We're about to get started on our fair projects."

"Good!" Courtney said. "I've bought something special to show you two." She placed a small wooden box on the table. Jessie smiled when she saw what was inside.

"Look at all the beautiful beads," Jessie said as she scooped up a handful.

"I've never seen anything like them," Violet said. "I love the colors." She held a small purple bead in her hand. It sparkled in the sunlight.

"These beads were made in Africa," Courtney explained. "My parents brought them back for me when they visited there. I thought we could make a beaded necklace and earrings like some African women wear. Then we could enter them in the fair."

"That's a wonderful idea," Jessie said.

"Have you decided what you're going to paint, Violet?" Courtney asked.

"I finished the sketch last night," Violet said.

"I'd love to see it," Courtney said.

Violet opened her sketchbook and showed the drawing to Courtney. It was a vase, filled with flowers of all types, sitting on a small wooden table near a window.

"That's going to be lovely," Courtney said.

"Thank you," Violet said. "I'm hoping one of us wins first place, then we can buy Grandfather's surprise birthday present."

"Oh, so that's why you all want to win so much," Courtney said, smiling. "That's a wonderful way to use the prize money."

"He's always doing something nice for us," Jessie explained. "We want to do something special for him."

"Well, let's get started," Courtney said. "The sooner we finish, the sooner we can enter the contest."

Violet set up her easel by the door, where the light was good. Jessie and Courtney arranged and rearranged the beads until they made just the right combination. The girls worked all morning on their projects.

"Look, Violet," Jessie said. "We're finished with our necklace."

"Oh," Violet said. "It's beautiful."

"We need to buy some more silver wire before we can finish the earrings," Jessie said.

"You're right," Courtney said. "There's only enough left to make one earring."

"I need to go to the crafts store, too," Violet said. "I'm just about out of yellow paint."

The girls walked into town to the crafts store. Jessie and Courtney followed Violet over to the art supplies aisle.

"Here it is," Violet said. "Shimmery Yel-

low #7. Can you see the little bits of metallic paper mixed in with the paint?"

"I've never seen paint like that before," Courtney said.

"It's new," Violet explained. "The metallic paper helps to reflect the light. It makes the paint look like sunshine. I'm going to use it to put the finishing touches on the flowers in my painting. The best thing about this paint is that as long as it's still wet, it's easy to remove. That way, if you make a mistake, you can still fix it."

"Your painting is going to be beautiful, Violet," Jessie said. "Come on. Let's find the wire we need to finish those earrings."

An older woman and a young girl blocked the end of the art supplies aisle. The girl carried a beautifully embroidered book bag with the initials KGS on it.

"Kristie, decide what paints you're going to use and do it quickly," the woman demanded. "I want to make sure you have everything you need to win that art contest at the fair."

"Mother, I really don't want to enter another contest," the girl said sadly. "I hate art competitions. It takes all the fun out of painting."

"Fun!" the woman said loudly. "I'm spending a lot of money on art lessons for you, and you seem to care only about painting for fun?"

"Mother, I don't like to paint if I can't enjoy myself," Kristie said softly.

"Pick out the supplies you need and let's go," her mother replied firmly. "You have to be finished with your painting today. I want to make sure it has time to dry before you enter it in the fair."

"Excuse us," Violet said. Then she recognized the girl and smiled. "Hello there, Kristie. Jessie and Courtney, this is a classmate, Kristie Stephens."

"Hello," Kristie said. "Nice to see you again, Violet. This is my mother."

Mrs. Stephens whirled around and frowned as she stared at Violet.

"I remember you, Violet," Kristie's mother said. "You won the art competition last year at school. Kristie came in fourth."

"Kristie's painting was lovely," Violet said.

"Well, the judges seemed to like your painting much better," Mrs. Stephens said. "Kristie has been taking art lessons, and her work has really improved. Hasn't it, Kristie?"

"I guess so, Mother," Kristie said.

"Are you entering the art competition at the fair, Violet?" Mrs. Stephens asked.

"Yes, I'd planned to," Violet said.

"Well, so is Kristie," Mrs. Stephens replied. "But this time, things are to be different."

"Well, good luck, Kristie," Violet said. "I'll see you at the fair."

Before Kristie could say good-bye, her mother took her arm and steered her up the aisle and out of the store.

"Goodness," Jessie said. "I really feel sorry for poor Kristie."

"Mrs. Stephens really wants Kristie to win the fair competition," Courtney said.

"I know," Violet said. "But Kristie didn't look like she was looking forward to it at all."

"Well, girls," Courtney said. "I see the wire we need for the earrings over there. We'd better hurry if we're going to finish our projects today."

The girls picked up the silver wire and paid for their supplies. Then they returned to the boxcar and unwrapped their purchases. Jessie and Courtney carefully began stringing the beautiful African beads on the thin silver wire. Finally, the earrings were finished. Courtney tried on the necklace.

"You look like an African princess," Jessie said.

"Thank you," Courtney said. "This necklace makes me feel like royalty. Maybe one of my ancestors *was* a princess."

"I hope the judges are impressed with our work," Jessie said. "If they are, we're sure to win the $25 prize."

CHAPTER 4

The Blueberry Pies

Violet was hard at work on her painting when Michael and Benny climbed inside the boxcar.

"Come and see our pies!" Michael said happily. "We're going to eat one of them after lunch."

"Just a minute, Michael," Violet said, "I'm almost finished."

"Hurry," Benny said. "Mrs. McGregor said we can't eat lunch without you."

"Oh," Courtney said with a laugh. "So that's the real reason you want us to hurry."

Benny grabbed Courtney's and Violet's hands. Michael held hands with Jessie. The children ran to the house as fast as they could go.

"Hi," Mrs. McGregor said as she wiped her hands on her apron. "I hope you've had as much fun with your projects as we've had with our pies."

"We sure have!" Jessie said.

"I was just about to take our pies out of the oven," Henry said.

"They smell delicious," Violet said.

"I can't wait to taste it," Jessie said.

"I'm not going to just taste my pie," Benny said. "I'm going to eat a big piece!"

Henry carefully covered his hands with a pair of oven mitts. Then he took one of the pies out of the oven. One side of the pie stood up just right. The other side was flat.

"Oh, my," Mrs. McGregor said. "The crust must have fallen down when you put it into the oven."

"I'm sure the second one looks better," Henry said.

He took the second pie out of the oven.

The juice from the blueberries had bubbled up through the crust. It was a sticky mess.

"Oh, no," Benny cried. "Our pie is ruined!"

Henry, Michael, and Benny looked very disappointed.

"I'm sure they taste wonderful," Courtney said.

"If you turn the first pie a certain way you hardly notice that one side is up and the other is down," Jessie said helpfully.

"I don't think it will win looking the way it does," Henry said.

"Just try and see," Courtney said. "You never know until you try."

"Anything that smells that good is bound to taste good," Violet said.

"I'm sure your pie will do just fine in the competition," Mrs. McGregor said. "Now, let's have lunch."

The children quickly finished their lunch. Then Henry cut a slice of the second pie for each of them.

"This pie is wonderful," Courtney said. "Good job, boys!"

"See, I told you," Jessie said. "It smells good and it tastes good, too!"

"Thank you," Michael said. "We worked hard on our pies, didn't we, Benny?"

"We sure did," Benny agreed.

"We couldn't have done it without Mrs. McGregor's help," Henry said.

"I'm proud of all of you," Mrs. McGregor said.

The next morning, the Alden children waited restlessly on their front steps for Courtney and Michael to arrive. Jessie had carefully placed the jewelry in layers of tissue paper. Violet had wrapped her painting in heavy brown paper. It rested beside her on the step. Henry and Benny had their blueberry pie in a bakery box.

"Where could they be?" Jessie asked. "If we don't hurry we'll miss the sign-up time for the competition."

"Here they come," Benny shouted.

"I'm sorry we're late," Courtney said as she ran up the stairs. "Michael insisted upon having seconds of everything at breakfast."

"It's a long time until lunch," Michael said. "I was worried there wouldn't be anything to eat at the fair."

"Oh, they have lots of good things to eat," Benny said. "I remember the fair we had last year."

"We remember it, too," Henry said. "You ate so much cotton candy you had an upset stomach."

"I won't eat too much cotton candy this year," Benny promised.

"I'll eat half of whatever he buys," Michael said helpfully. "That way, he can't eat too much."

"Thank you, Michael," Henry said. "That sounds like a good plan."

The high school marching band was playing a merry tune when the children arrived at the fairgrounds. Brightly colored tents with signs that said EXHIBITS, FOOD, DRINKS, GAMES, BAKED GOODS CONTEST, CRAFTS CONTEST, and ART CONTEST lined the walkway. Crowds of adults and children moved from tent to tent. Screams and laughter from the roller coaster and Ferris wheel could be faintly heard. The smell of roasted peanuts, popcorn, and hot dogs filled the air.

"I love the county fair," Henry said. "This is one of my favorite times of the year."

"I love it, too," Jessie said.

"There's the contest registration booth," Courtney said as she pointed to the bright red sign.

"Good," Violet said. "This painting is getting heavy."

"Can we go over there and ride on the carousel?" Michael asked.

"Yeah!" Benny said. "I want to ride on that big white horse."

"Just wait, you two," Henry said. "I'd better go with you. You have to buy tickets first."

"I'll register the pie for you," Jessie said. "If there's a problem, I'll come and get you."

"Thanks," Henry said. "We'll meet you at the bumper cars in half an hour."

"Behave yourself, Benny," Jessie said.

"You, too, Michael," Courtney said.

"We will," the boys said as they dashed off. Henry ran to catch up with them.

As the girls neared the registration desk they heard angry voices. A man wearing a badge that said JUDGE was patiently explaining something to a woman wearing a bright red dress.

"Rules are rules," the woman shouted. "The poster said that all entries must be accompanied by an official form."

"I know that, ma'am," the judge said. "But several people have complained that they couldn't find any posters with entry forms. I don't know what happened to them. We posted at least fifty posters around the town. We had to change the rules or we wouldn't have had enough people to hold a contest."

"That's not fair," the woman said. "We had to fill out three entry forms! One for my lemon poundcake, one for my needlepoint pillow, and one for my daughter's painting. Anyone without an official form shouldn't be allowed to enter the contests."

"Where did you find that form?" the judge

asked. "Everyone else seemed to have trouble locating them."

"What difference does that make?" the woman said. "We are entering the contest according to the rules."

"Ma'am," the judge said, "why don't you talk with the contest officials over at the crafts booth? Maybe they can help you."

"I'll do just that," the woman said. "But believe me, this is not the end of this matter." Then she stomped off.

"Wasn't that Kristie Stephens's mother?" Jessie asked Violet.

"Yes," Violet said. "Boy, she sure was upset."

"What was that all about?" Jessie asked the judge.

"Just some troublemaker," the judge said. "We're not going to let her ruin the contests for everyone just because most of the entry forms around town disappeared."

"Really?" Jessie said. "We managed to get a few. But when we returned to get some more for our friends, the poster had been torn up."

"Why would someone want to tear up the entry forms?" Courtney asked.

"We've been wondering that ourselves," the judge said. "There's been one problem after another ever since the contests were announced."

"How strange," Jessie said. "Is someone trying to make sure that no one enters the contests?"

"That could be," the judge said. He carefully checked their entry forms and stamped them. "Now, I need for you to sign that form on the table over there. Then you will be officially entered in the County Fair."

The girls stood in line at the sign-in table behind a pretty girl with long blond hair.

"Oh, great," the girl said as she shook her pen. "This pen is all out of ink."

"I've got one," Jessie said. She handed the girl a pen. Then she glanced down at the girl's name on the sign-in sheet. "Susie?"

"Yes," the girl replied. "Susie Martinilli is my name. It's nice to meet you."

"It's nice to meet you, too. I'm Jessie Al-

den and this is my sister, Violet, and our
friend Courtney Jenkins."

The girls exchanged greetings. Susie finished signing in. The girls noticed that she
dotted the i's in her name with tiny hearts.

"Thanks so much for letting me use your
pen," Susie said as she handed it back to
Jessie.

"You're welcome," Jessie said. Then she
signed everyone up for the contests.

"What contests are you entering?" Susie
asked.

"I'm entering my painting in the art contest," Violet said.

"May I see it?" Susie asked.

"Sure," Violet said. She loosened the
brown wrapping paper and held the painting
up for Susie to see.

"That's very nice," Susie said. "That yellow paint you used is beautiful."

"Thank you," Violet said. "It's a new paint
I found at the crafts store."

"Jessie and I made a necklace and earrings
out of some African beads," Courtney said.
She showed the jewelry to Susie.

"How beautiful," Susie said. "It looks like the whole thing is held together by this wire string. Is that right?"

"Yes," Jessie said. "It's not that hard to make."

"What's in that bakery box?" Susie asked.

"Oh, that's a blueberry pie our brothers made," Violet said.

"Well," Susie said. "It looks like you've entered every event at the fair! So did I."

"You entered every event?" Jessie said.

"Yes, I did," Susie said with a laugh. "I just love competition."

"How many times have you entered?" Courtney asked.

"I've entered every year for the last eight years," Susie said. "But I've never won anything. So this year I made a cherry pie for the baked goods contest, a rag rug for the crafts contest, and I painted a picture of a horse for the art competition."

"You've really worked hard," Violet said. "Maybe you'll have better luck this year."

"I hope so," Susie said. "I think my chances are much better this time. For some reason, not that many people are competing this year."

"That's because someone tore down all the posters announcing the contests," Jessie explained.

"Really?" Susie said. "How strange."

Just then, the man in the baseball cap the Aldens had seen in front of the fair poster the other day entered the registration tent. He looked at the sign-in sheet carefully and made notes on a small pad. When he noticed Violet was watching him, he hurried off.

"There's that man who was asking us so many questions," Violet said.

"I wonder what he's up to now," Jessie said.

"I don't know," Violet said. "But the moment he saw us he rushed off."

"Maybe we can figure out what's going on before the fair is over," Jessie said.

"I'm sure it's nothing serious," Susie said. "Excuse me, but there's something I have to do before the contests start."

"Well, it was nice meeting you," Courtney said.

"Good luck," Violet said.

"Yes," Jessie said. "Good luck. We'll see you this afternoon."

"Let's drop our projects off at the contest tents," Courtney said when Susie had gone. "Then we can go meet the boys at the bumper cars."

"That's a good idea," Violet said. "We've got a couple of hours before the pie competition starts."

"I want to ride the bumper cars first, then the Ferris wheel, and then the roller coaster," Jessie said.

"I can't believe you want to ride the roller coaster again the way you screamed last year," Violet said.

"I really wasn't scared," Jessie said. "I was just teasing you."

"Well, you did a good job," Violet said. "I thought you were terrified."

"I love riding on the roller coaster, too," Courtney said.

"Great," Jessie said, as she smiled at her friend. "We can scream together."

The girls laughed and headed toward the

contest tents. First, they stopped at the baked goods tent. They received tag number six from the judge. Jessie put the boys' blueberry pie next to a chocolate cake. Then she placed the tag in front of it. The boys' blueberry pie looked even more lopsided than it had the day before.

"Oh, well," Jessie said. "We know it tastes much better than it looks."

"I don't see Susie's cherry pie," Courtney said.

"Maybe she's dropping off her other projects first," Violet said. "Come on, I want to see the other paintings in the art competition."

"I can't wait to see the other crafts projects," Courtney said.

"I want to see them, too," Jessie said. "Let's go."

CHAPTER 5

Fun at the Fair

The girls hurried over to the art competition tent. Four paintings were already displayed. Violet picked up tag number five.

"Has Kristie Stephens or Susie Martinilli entered their paintings yet?" Violet asked the judge.

"Yes, I'm sure they have," the judge said. "Although I'm not sure which one is which. We usually have more than twenty entries in this contest. But we've only had about half that many this year. I can't understand why more people didn't participate."

The girls exchanged glances.

"The judging for the art contest will be at 1:00 tomorrow," the judge said.

The girls looked at each one of the paintings on display. Then Violet noticed a book bag with the initials KGS underneath one of the easels.

"This must be Kristie's artwork," Violet said. "These are her initials on the book bag." Kristie had painted a beautiful multicolored sunset. "She did a wonderful job."

"It is good," Courtney agreed.

"This must be Susie's painting," Jessie said when she reached the fourth entry. "She said that she painted a picture of a horse. I like her work, too."

Susie's portrait of a chestnut brown horse galloping across an emerald green field was also lovely.

"It's a beautiful painting," Courtney said.

"It sure is," Jessie agreed.

"This is going to be a good competition," Violet said as she placed her painting on an easel.

"Your work is every bit as good as the other entries here," Courtney said. "It's still my favorite."

"Thank you," Violet said. "I really worked hard on it."

"We'd better go over to the crafts tent now," Jessie said.

When they arrived at the crafts tent, Courtney picked up tag number three. She carefully placed the beaded necklace on the display table. Jessie put the earrings beside it.

"I can hardly wait until this afternoon to see what the judges think," Courtney said.

Suddenly, a loudspeaker blared out. "Attention, everyone, the Grand Opening Celebration of the Greenfield County Fair will begin at 12:00 noon at the main pavilion."

"We'd better hurry if we're going to go on any rides before the celebration begins," Jessie said.

The girls made their way through the milling crowd toward the bumper cars. They could hear Benny and Michael before they saw them. The boys' laughter and excited voices rose above the music of the fair.

"There they are," Violet said.

Michael and Benny were having a wonderful time steering a bright yellow bumper car. They were busily ramming into the side of Henry's car.

"Back up, Michael," Benny said. "Let's do it again."

"Help me," Henry said when he noticed the girls leaning over the railing.

"I'm afraid you'll have to get out of this one on your own," Jessie said.

Henry turned the wheel of his car sharply and sped away from the two little boys. They followed him, laughing all the way. Before the boys could bump Henry again the cars slowed to a stop.

"Everyone please exit to your left," the ride operator announced. "Thank you for your cooperation."

"Safe at last," Henry said as he got out of the car.

"Let's do it again," Benny said.

"You'll have to wait, Benny," Violet said. "It's our turn now."

"Why don't you boys ride on the Super Swing over there while you're waiting," Courtney suggested. "Then afterward we can all ride the Ferris wheel."

"Good idea!" Michael said. The two little boys quickly ran over to the Super Swing.

"Wait for me," Henry said.

The girls each chose a bumper car to ride.

"Please fasten your seat belts," the ride operator announced. He walked around checking each car to be sure everyone was fastened in safely. Then he threw the switch and the ride began.

Courtney immediately rammed her sporty red bumper car into the back of Violet's blue one.

"Oh," Violet said, laughing. "I didn't see that one coming."

She chased Courtney around the track until she was rammed sideways by Jessie. Laughing loudly, Jessie tried to speed away.

The girls chased each other around and around the track. After many collisions and a lot of laughter, they heard the ride operator, say "Thank you for riding the bumper cars. Please exit to your left."

"I love riding the bumper cars," Courtney said. "It's one of my favorite amusement park rides."

"Well, now it's time for my favorite ride," Jessie said. "Let's get the boys and go over to the Ferris wheel."

After buying their tickets and waiting in line, the children climbed into their seats on the Ferris wheel. Benny and Michael sat together, and Violet and Henry shared a car. Jessie and Courtney were behind them. The ride operator checked to make sure the metal bar was secure across their laps and then started the ride.

"I love the Ferris wheel," Jessie said, "especially when they stop the ride at the top."

When the cars reached the top of the Ferris wheel the children could see all over the fairgrounds. The cars paused and slowly came down again. The ride was over much too quickly. The children climbed out of the cars and then ran over to get their tickets for the roller coaster.

"Sorry," the ride operator said when he

saw Benny and Michael. "No one six or under can ride the roller coaster."

"That's okay," Benny said. "I'm ready to eat now anyway."

"Me, too," Michael said.

"I'm hungry, too," Violet said. "I'll take them over to get a hot dog while you three ride the roller coaster."

"Okay," Jessie said.

"After we ride the roller coaster, it will be time for the Grand Opening Celebration," Henry said. "Why don't we meet you at the main tent?"

"We'll wait for you there," Violet said.

When it was their turn, Jessie, Courtney, and Henry eagerly climbed onto the roller coaster. The cars slowly pulled up to the peak of a large hill. They stopped there for a moment. Then, suddenly, the cars hurled down the tracks at full speed.

"Eeeeek!" screamed Courtney. "This is a really steep hill."

Jessie clutched the safety bar tightly. Ahead the long track dipped down again, then went up into a double loop. "I can't

look," Jessie shrieked, closing her eyes.

"Hang on," Henry called to the girls. "Here we go!"

At lightning speed the cars whipped around the first loop. Then they went down a straight stretch of tracks and whipped around the second loop.

The children screamed and laughed as the cars rounded the tracks. The train zipped around several curves. Then it dropped into a steep, heart-pounding dive, and at last slowly pulled into the boarding platform again.

"I don't know if I can walk," Courtney said as she leaned on Jessie for support. "My legs are trembling."

"Wasn't it great?" Henry said.

"Yes!" Jessie said. "I wasn't scared at all."

"You said that last year, too," Henry said.

"Well," Jessie said. "This year I kept my eyes closed the whole time so I couldn't see anything."

"Come on, you two," Courtney said with a laugh. "We need to go if we're going to find Violet, Benny, and Michael before the grand opening begins."

The children hurried down the ramp and headed toward the big tent in the center of the fair.

It hadn't taken long for Violet, Benny, and Michael to find a hot dog stand. The two little boys followed their noses to the bright yellow cart. Violet had to run to catch up with them.

"Hurry up, Violet," Benny called. "We've already ordered."

"I'd like one hot dog with mustard, please," Violet told the hot dog man. "And three containers of apple juice."

"We ordered ketchup on our hot dogs," Michael said. "I love ketchup."

"There you are," the man said with a smile. He handed each one of them a hot dog.

The children paid for their lunches, then found seats at a small table. Violet was almost finished eating when she saw Kristie

Stephens run out of the baked good competition tent.

"Hi, Kristie," Violet said. "Come join us."

"No, I can't," Kristie called back. "I have
to find my mother."

"Will you be at the opening celebration?"
Violet asked. "Maybe we can sit together."

"I don't know," Kristie said. She looked
troubled. "I'm sorry. I really need to go
now."

"All right," Violet said. "See you later."

"What was the matter with her, Violet?"
Benny asked.

"I don't know, Benny," Violet said.
"Maybe we'll find out later."

"I'm all finished," Michael said as he wiped
his mouth. "Can we go to the opening celebration now?"

"Sure, let's go," Violet said.

Someone on a loudspeaker was announcing the start of the celebration just as Violet
and the boys entered the open tent. Violet
scanned the bleachers for the others.

"Here we are," Jessie said, waving to her

sister. "We had a wonderful time on the roller coaster."

The children quickly found seats near the top of the bleachers. Then the opening ceremonies began!

The Greenfield High School Marching Band started up a merry tune and began marching around the arena. The Greenfield Majorettes threw their batons in the air two at a time. When they finished, the crowd gave them a standing ovation.

The majorettes joined the band as they marched in and out of several formations.

"Look," Benny said. "They're spelling out something. G-R-E-E-N-F-I-E-L-D."

"That spells Greenfield!" Michael said.

"That's right," Jessie said as she smiled at the two little boys.

The Greenfield marching band finished their performance with another lively tune; then they marched over to one side of the arena and continued to play.

The band was followed by several contest officials who were riding in a horse-drawn wagon. The judges waved to the crowd as the wagon circled the arena. A livestock display was the last event. Grown-ups and children slowly walked their horses, cows, sheep, and pigs around and around the arena. The band played another tune and then the grand opening was over. The mayor walked to the center of the arena and picked up the microphone again.

"Thank you all again for coming to the Greenfield County Fair," the mayor said. "I have just a few announcements. The baked goods competition begins at 12:30. The craft competition begins at 1:30. Tomorrow morning at 10:00 A.M. will be the grand opening of the livestock show. Then the art competition will began at 1:00 P.M. Welcome again, one and all, and let's have a good time at the fair!"

Immediately after the mayor finished her announcements, hundreds of balloons were released from the ceiling.

"We'd better hurry over to the baked goods tent," Henry said. "I want to get a front row seat."

"Me, too," Courtney said. "This is so exciting. I'm glad you told us about the fair."

CHAPTER 6

The Competition

When the children arrived at the baked good competition, a large crowd was gathered outside the tent. Many people were yelling, and the judges were trying to calm down the crowd.

"I wonder what's wrong," Jessie said.

"There's Susie," Violet said. "Maybe she knows."

The children worked their way through the crowd until they reached Susie's side.

"Hi, Susie," Jessie said. "Do you know what's going on here?"

"I'm not sure," Susie said. "But I think something happened to the baked goods that were entered in the competition."

"Oh, no," Benny said. "What happened to our pie?"

"Did someone eat it?" Michael asked.

"I don't think so, Michael," Henry said. "Look, there are the judges. I think they're going to explain what happened."

The three judges whispered among themselves for a while. Then, one of them stepped forward. He held up his hands to quiet the crowd.

"Folks," the judge began, "I have some sad news about the baked goods competition. It seems that someone has deliberately damaged most of the contest entries. Out of a total of seven entries, two cakes and three pies were damaged."

"Oh, no," someone who was standing behind Violet said. Violet turned around. She came face to face with Kristie Stephens and her mother.

"I can't imagine why anyone would do such a thing," Violet said. "Can you?"

Kristie stared at the ground. Her face was beet red.

"Attention, please, everyone," the judge said. "The contest officials have asked me to announce that they are offering a reward. Fifty dollars will be given to anyone who provides information leading to the identity of the person or persons who have been damaging the property and entries in the Greenfield County Fair."

"I certainly hope that my lemon cake wasn't damaged," Mrs. Stephens called out. "I worked very hard on the frosting."

"I'm sure all the contestants worked hard on their entries," the judge said. "We apologize for this awful turn of events. Unless we think of something quickly, the contest will have to be canceled."

The Aldens and Courtney and Michael began to whisper among themselves. Then Jessie raised her hand. "We have an idea that might work," she said.

"Yes," the judge said. "What's your suggestion?"

"Maybe the contest could be for the best-

tasting baked goods. No matter how they look," Jessie said.

"That's a great idea," the judge said, smiling. "The contest will be judged on taste alone. The appearance of the baked goods will not matter. Let's start the competition!"

The crowd began to applaud. The judge threw open the tent flaps to let everyone in.

As the crowd filled the stands, the children gathered around the display table. Someone had poked holes in the boys' blueberry pie.

"Look at our pie," Benny said sadly. "Why would anyone do something so mean?"

"We'll probably never win now," Michael said.

"Don't worry, boys," Courtney said. "You heard the judge, looks don't matter anymore. Let's go find a seat so the judges can start the contest."

The children found seats in the bleachers. Henry leaned over to talk to Jessie.

"I think I know who might have done this," Henry whispered to Jessie.

"Who?" Jessie whispered back.

"Look over there by the entrance to the

tent," Henry said. "It's that man in the base-ball cap again."

Jessie nudged Violet when she spotted the man in the baseball cap. He was looking in their direction.

"I see him now," Violet said.

"What are you looking at?" Courtney asked.

"The man who was asking us so many questions the other day is standing near the front of the tent," Jessie explained.

"He always seems to show up when trouble's around," Violet said.

"Let's talk about this later. The contest is about to begin," Henry said.

Each judge picked up a plate and a fork. They gathered around pie number one, cutting it into small slices, and each one took a bite. Then they whispered among themselves and wrote something down on a clipboard.

"I don't think they liked it that much," Michael whispered.

"How can you tell?" Benny asked.

"They didn't lick their forks," Michael said.

Then the judges sampled Mrs. Stephens's lemon cake. It had not been damaged. The cake was beautifully frosted and it looked especially nice compared to the other entries. The judges cut slices of the cake, tasted it, and discussed it in whispers. One judge began to smile.

"They seem to really like Mrs. Stephens's cake," Violet said.

"Wait a minute," Jessie said. "Now they're cutting the blueberry pie."

The judges lingered near the pie, whispering among themselves. Then they tasted the pie again!

"They like it!" Benny said.

The judges made notes on their clipboard. Then they moved down to Susie's cherry pie. It was the only other entry that hadn't been damaged. The judges tasted the pie and made a few notes. Then they huddled together for a few moments, talking and waving their hands.

After a while, one of the judges stepped up to the microphone and read from his clipboard.

"The winner of the Greenfield County Fair Baked Goods Competition is entry number six! Henry and Benny Alden and Michael Jenkins. They will share the $25 First Prize! Will the winners please come over to the awards stand!"

"Hooray!" Jessie shouted as the boys walked up to the front of the tent.

Courtney and Violet hugged each other and clapped their hands. The crowd broke out in a round of applause.

He gave a beautiful trophy to Michael and a blue ribbon to Benny. Then the judge presented the envelope to Henry.

"Here's the prize money," the judge said. "Congratulations."

"Thank you all very much," Henry said.

"Thank you," Michael said as he admired the trophy.

"Thank you," Benny said. "This was fun."

"Ladies and gentlemen," the judge announced. "The judging of the crafts will begin at 1:30. Please join us there."

The crowd began to slowly file out of the tent. One of the judges also started to leave.

When Mrs. Stephens saw him, she pushed her way through the crowd.

"Mr. Judge," shouted Mrs. Stephens. "I'd like to have a word with you. This contest was not held in accordance with the rules. My cake should have received extra points for looking so good." She followed the judge, talking loudly and waving her hands excitedly.

"Oh, no," Courtney said. "Mrs. Stephens is at it again."

"I wonder where Kristie is," Violet said. "She was here before the contest started. I saw her when I was eating lunch but then she disappeared."

"That's strange," Jessie said. "You'd think she'd want to be here since her mother was part of the competition."

"This whole contest has been very peculiar," Violet said.

The girls hurried over to congratulate the prizewinners.

"Now, you see," Jessie said as she hugged Benny. "I told you that pie was a prizewinner."

"Congratulations, boys," Courtney said.

"I'm proud of all of you," Violet said.

"Thank you," Benny said. "Can we eat the rest of the pie now?"

"Of course," the judge said with a laugh. "I think I'll have another piece myself. That's one of the best blueberry pies I have ever tasted."

"You seemed to enjoy Mrs. Stephens's lemon cake, too," Henry said.

"No, I was very disappointed by that cake," the judge said.

"Why?" Violet asked. "It looks so pretty."

"Yes, it is a beautiful cake," the judge agreed. "But it tastes awful. This blueberry pie isn't very pretty, but it tastes wonderful!"

Everyone laughed. The judge cut a slice of pie for each one of them.

"We'd better go now," Jessie said when everyone finished eating. "The crafts contest will be starting soon."

The children arrived at the crafts tent a few minutes before the contest started. Mrs. Stephens was talking to the judge. She had Susie's rag rug in her hand.

"As you can see," Mrs. Stephens said as she pointed to the rug, "a sewing machine was used to make these stitches. The rules state that every entry in the crafts competition must be handmade or hand-sewn. I have a copy of the rules right here."

"I know the rules," the judge said. He examined the rug. Then he called for Susie to come forward. Susie talked with the judge for a few moments. She looked very upset. She folded her rug and ran out of the tent.

"I'm going to see if she's all right," Jessie said.

"We'll save you a seat," Henry said as the other children began to climb up the bleachers.

Jessie found Susie sitting outside on a bench.

"What's the matter, Susie?" Jessie asked. "Why are you taking your rug out of the competition?"

"Mrs. Stephens had me disqualified because I used a sewing machine!" Susie said. "I didn't even know about this rule. I'm so disappointed. I was hoping that my rug would win that event."

Suddenly, Jessie noticed the man with the baseball cap. He was staring at them and writing something in a small notebook.

"There's that man again," Jessie said.

"Who is he?" Susie said. "I saw him at the pie contest, too."

"I wonder what he's up to now," Jessie said. "He always seems to be around whenever there's some trouble."

The man glanced at the girls and quickly walked in the other direction.

"I'm sure it's just a coincidence," Susie said. "You better go now. The contest will be starting soon."

"Maybe you'll have better luck with your painting," Jessie said. "It's lovely."

"Thanks," Susie said. "It's my last chance to win."

Jessie returned to the tent and explained what had happened to Susie.

"How awful," Violet said. "She must have really worked hard on her rug."

"I think we'd better check our necklace and earrings," Courtney said. "After everything that's happened today, I'm afraid someone may have been up to more mischief."

Courtney reached the exhibit table first. She picked up one of the earrings. It seemed to be fine. But when Jessie picked up the necklace, the beads began to slip off.

"Oh, no!" Courtney said. "Someone has cut through the wire that holds the necklace together." She held the jagged ends of the necklace up so that Jessie could see them.

"What are we going to do," Jessie said as she reached for the missing beads. "The contest starts in five minutes!"

"I know what we can do," Violet said. "I have a miniature sewing kit in my purse. Maybe we can string the loose beads together with thread."

"It's worth a try," Courtney said.

"Here's the sewing kit," Violet said. "I'll go and explain what happened to the judge. Maybe they can delay the contest for a few moments."

Violet talked to the judges. They nodded as she told them what had happened. One judge, a lady in a large flowered hat, addressed the crowd.

"Ladies and gentlemen," the judge announced. "The contest will be delayed for five minutes. Please remain seated. Thank you."

Courtney and Jessie frantically worked on the necklace.

"I'm sure glad Violet had this sewing kit," Jessie said, as she strung the last bead.

"Me, too," Courtney said.

"Good as new," Jessie said as she held up the newly repaired necklace. "I'll take it back to the exhibition table."

The contest finally began. The judges slowly examined each one of the crafts entries. Courtney and Jessie held their breath when they reached the necklace and earrings.

"I hope that thread holds," Courtney whispered to her friend.

"I'm sure everything is going to be just fine," Jessie said. But she still looked worried.

CHAPTER 7

Trouble at the Fair

After the judges looked at all the craft entries, they huddled together for a long time. The judge with the flowered hat and a tall judge seemed to disagree on something. They walked back to Mrs. Stephens's needlepoint pillow and examined it closely. Then they moved down to the African necklace and earrings. They picked up the earrings. The beads sparkled in the light.

"Oh, my goodness," Courtney whispered to Jessie. "What if they pick up the necklace again and it breaks?"

"We tied it pretty tightly," Jessie whispered back. "I'm sure the knots will hold."

"Look at Mrs. Stephens over there," Violet said. "She's just as nervous as we are."

Mrs. Stephens was seated in the front row. She was twisting a lacy handkerchief tightly in her hands. Her eyes followed the judges' every move. Kristie was seated beside her. She patted her mother on the arm.

The judges went back and forth between the pillow and the jewelry for a few minutes. Finally, the third judge stepped forward to the microphone.

"Ladies and gentlemen," the judge said. "We appreciate your patience. Unfortunately, the judges have not been able to reach a unanimous decision on the winner of the crafts contest. As you know, there can only be one winner in each category. At the present time, the judges have narrowed their choices down to the needlepoint pillow, submitted by Mrs. Kathy Stephens, and the African necklace and earrings, submitted by Jessie Alden and Courtney Jenkins."

Jessie and Courtney smiled at each other.

"I'm so excited for you both," Violet whispered.

"According to the contest rules, no ties are allowed," the judge continued. "We are asking for a thirty-minute recess while we privately examine each entry. Afterward, we will consult with a contest official and re-tally all the points. We'd appreciate it if everyone would exit as quickly and as quietly as possible. Thank you again for your patience. Enjoy the fair."

Everyone began filing out of the tent and into the bright sunshine.

"Well, I never," Jessie heard Mrs. Stephens say. "All this waiting and we still don't know who the winner is."

"Mother," Kristie replied. "The judges just need a little more time in order to reach a decision."

"Well, nothing has been done properly during any of these competitions," Mrs. Stephens said. "It's simply not fair. I'm not going to put up with losing again just because these judges don't know the rules."

"Why don't we get something to eat while

we're waiting?" Kristie suggested. "It might make you feel better."

"All right," Mrs. Stephens said. "But after this event I'm going to go talk to the contest official. Something has to be done about these rules."

Jessie couldn't hear anything else because Kristie and her mother were soon lost in the crowd. Henry tapped her on the shoulder.

"Jessie, everybody's sitting over there," Henry said. He pointed to the other children who were seated underneath a tree.

"I'm sorry," Jessie said. "I was listening to Mrs. Stephens. She's really upset about the competition."

"One mysterious thing after another has happened at this fair," Henry said. "Tonight let's see if we can put our heads together and find out why."

"That's a good idea," Jessie said. "I know that there must be a reason for all this trouble."

"Maybe we can all try to think of every suspicious thing we've seen and heard while we've been here," Henry suggested. "Then we might be able to solve this mystery."

Henry and Jessie ran to join the other children. They were trying to decide what to do while they waited for the judges' decision.

"Let's enter the sack race!" Benny said. "That was fun last year."

"That's a good idea," Jessie said. "I love the sack races."

"Do they give prizes for the sack race?" Michael asked.

"No," Violet said. "It's just for fun."

"Let's go!" Benny said.

The sack races were held in a large field next to the fair rides. Several children were already gathered around a pile of empty potato sacks.

"Whew," Courtney said as she held the top of her sack and tried to walk. "Moving around in this sack is harder than it looks."

"If you think this is hard," Jessie said, "just wait until the three-legged race starts."

When all the children had slipped on a sack, they waddled over to join the rest of the crowd.

"I feel like a duck," Benny said.

"Well," Courtney said. "You'll need to hop like a rabbit in order to win."

After everyone was in line, the contest began.

"Ready, Set, Go!" the judge said as he waved his arms to start the race.

Everyone began hopping toward the finish line. Benny was halfway across the field when, suddenly, he tripped. Michael stumbled over him. Jessie collided with Michael. Violet and Courtney landed in a pile next to her. Soon Henry was laughing so much he could hardly breathe. All the other children began to laugh with him.

"Well, at least no one is hurt," Henry said.

"Only my pride," Jessie said as she struggled to her feet. Henry helped her up.

"Let's try the three-legged race now," Violet said. "We had better luck with that race last year."

"I didn't fall down during the three-legged race," Benny said.

"Good," Michael said. "We can race together."

The children chose a brightly colored scarf

from a pile that was marked Three-Legged Race. Henry helped Benny and Michael tie their ankles together. Then he pulled them up on their feet. The two little boys practiced hopping around and around while they waited for the older children to get ready.

"This is fun!" Michael said happily.

Finally, the race began. Violet and Henry hopped along together, followed by Jessie and Courtney. Benny and Michael were behind a large group of adults at the beginning of the race. Suddenly, the two little boys began to move faster and faster. Before long, they had hopped past everyone else and crossed the finish line.

"Hooray for Michael and Benny!" the older children shouted.

"We beat you to the finish line," Benny said.

"We hopped as fast as we could," Michael explained. "That's how we won."

"Good job," Henry said as he untied their legs. "There's nothing like teamwork."

"I think we'd better get back to the craft competition tent now," Jessie said.

"Oh, I'm getting nervous again," Courtney said. "I was having so much fun, I forgot all about the competition."

"I wonder if the judges have reached a decision," Violet said.

"I'm sure they have by now," Henry said. "Let's go."

Most of the bleachers were filled by the time the children arrived. They found a place to sit near the top of the stands. The crowd whispered excitedly as the judges entered the tent. The judge with the flowered hat picked up the microphone.

"We are now ready to announce the winner," the judge said.

Courtney and Jessie held hands tightly. Violet held her breath. Mrs. Stephens began to twist her handkerchief again. She leaned forward anxiously as the judge read the winner.

"The winning entry in the Greenfield County Fair Crafts Competition is the African necklace and earrings which were made by Courtney Jenkins and Jessie Alden. Girls, please come over to the winner's table."

"You won, you won!" Benny and Michael said as they clapped the girls on the back. Cheers and applause rang out from the audience.

Violet hugged her sister and her friend. Courtney and Jessie walked down the aisle toward the winners' table. But as they approached the judges, they could see that something was terribly wrong.

"I can't believe this!" said one judge.

"It must be here," said the woman in the flowered hat."

"No — I've looked and looked," said the third judge. "The money and the trophy are gone." He turned to the girls. "I'm so sorry," the judge said. "It appears that someone has taken the trophy and the envelope that had the check for $25 in it!"

"Oh, no," Courtney said. "I can't believe this is happening." Her eyes filled with tears.

"It'll be all right, Courtney," Jessie said. "You'll see."

The judges whispered together for a moment. Then the lady with the flowered hat picked up the microphone. "Ladies and gentlemen," she began. "The trophy and prize money which were to be awarded to these young ladies is missing. The theft must have taken place while we were in the contest official's office. If anyone has any information on the identity of the person or persons who may have taken the prizes from the awards table, please contact us immediately."

Henry, Violet, Benny, and Michael worked their way through the crowd until they reached Jessie and Courtney.

"This is awful," Violet said.

"I can't believe someone would do something like this," Henry said. "I think we need to talk to the judges about what's been going on since the contests were announced."

"I think that's a good idea," Courtney said.

"May we talk with you for a moment?" Jessie asked the lady in the flowered hat.

"Certainly," she replied.

"Something very strange has been going on since the fair began," Jessie said. "But we haven't been able to figure it out."

"What do you mean?" another judge asked.

The children told the judges every suspicious thing they had seen and heard since the fair began.

"My goodness," the judge with the flowered hat said. "Imagine someone deliberately trying to ruin the fair contests!"

"Well, someone is," Henry said. "The question is who?"

"I know one thing," Violet said. "Whoever took the trophy and prize money didn't have very long to hide it."

"That's true," Jessie said. "They wouldn't be able to carry that trophy around without someone seeing them."

"Maybe," Violet said, "they hid it somewhere nearby. Then, after the fair, they could go back and get it."

"Let's look around," Henry said.

Just then, Jessie saw the man with the baseball cap near the entrance to the tent.

"There's that man again," Jessie whispered to the others. "I wonder how long he's been listening to us."

"What man?" one of the judges asked.

"It's that man in the baseball cap we told

you about," Jessie said. "Look, he just ran outside."

"Maybe if we hurry we can follow him," Henry said.

"Let's go," Jessie said.

The children hurried outside. They looked around carefully, but they couldn't find the man with the baseball cap in the crowd.

"He seems to have disappeared," Courtney said. "What are we going to do now?"

"I'll take the boys and we'll look all around the area in back of the tent for the missing trophy and prize money," Henry said. "Maybe the rest of you can search around the other sides."

Jessie said, "Let's meet in front of the tent in about ten minutes. If no one has found anything we'll spread out a little farther."

The children began searching the area around the crafts tent. After several minutes, the girls heard Benny calling their names.

"Violet, Jessie, and Courtney, come here," Benny said. "Look what we found!"

The girls ran as fast as they could to the

back of the crafts tent. Benny was holding a bag in one hand and the trophy in the other.

"Where did you find it?" Jessie asked.

"Someone stuffed it in this bag. It was partly hidden inside this empty box," Henry explained.

"We saw the trophy shining in the sun," Michael said.

"Let me see that bag, Benny," Violet said. "This looks like the bag Kristie was carrying at the crafts store."

"Look at the initials embroidered on the front of the bag," Courtney said. "KGS."

"Yes," Violet said. "Those are Kristie's initials. But I can't believe she'd do something like this."

"The judge said that Mrs. Stephens's first name is Kathy," Henry said. "This could be her bag and not Kristie's."

"Maybe," Jessie said. "But Kristie was holding the bag as if it were hers."

"Why do you think Kristie would take the trophy and the prize money?" Courtney asked.

"Let's see if we can find her and ask her

before we tell the judges about this," Jessie said. "Maybe she can explain what happened."

"Where do you think Kristie went?" Henry asked.

"Mrs. Stephens said earlier that she was going to talk with the contest official," Jessie said. "I'll bet we can find Kristie with her mother at the registration tent."

The children hurried to the bright red registration tent. They could hear Mrs. Stephens before they saw her. She was loudly complaining to the contest official about the rules.

"I demand an explanation for all this confusion," Mrs. Stephens was saying to the contest official.

"Mother, please," Kristie said. She looked like she wished she were somewhere else.

"Excuse us, Mrs. Stephens," Violet said. "We have something we need to talk to Kristie about."

"That's my bag!" Kristie said when she saw what Violet had in her hand.

"We found it inside one of the boxes that

were stacked behind the crafts tent," Jessie explained.

"What was it doing there?" Kristie asked. She opened up the bag and looked inside.

Violet watched Kristie's face carefully. Kristie looked very shocked when she saw the trophy and prize money inside her bag.

"Young lady," the contest official said. "You have a lot of explaining to do."

"I don't know how that trophy or that envelope got inside my bag," Kristie said.

"This is outrageous," Mrs. Stephens complained loudly.

"Did you misplace your bag somewhere?" Violet asked.

"Maybe someone found it and used it to hide the trophy and envelope inside. That way, it would look like you were the one who took them," Courtney said.

"I left my bag in the art competition tent this morning," Kristie said. "I had my paint supplies in it."

Kristie dug inside the bag.

"See," she said as she held up several tubes of paint and a brush, "my supplies are still inside." Kristie looked close to tears.

"Well," the contest official said, "the fact remains that someone stole the trophy and prize money."

"It wasn't me," Kristie said. "I would never do anything like that."

"Did you see anyone else around the tent while you were there?" Jessie asked.

"Yes," Kristie said. "Two people were there. A girl I didn't know, and a man with a baseball cap."

"What did the girl look like?" Violet asked.

"No more questions!" Mrs. Stephens interrupted. "We've been through quite enough for one day. We're going home!"

Mrs. Stephens took Kristie by the arm and hurried off.

CHAPTER 8

The Man with the Baseball Cap

That evening, the Aldens gathered in the boxcar to talk. The Jenkins children had divided the prize money evenly with the Aldens. Courtney and Michael took a trophy and a blue ribbon home with them. The other trophy and blue ribbon were on the shelf that Jessie and Violet had made in the boxcar.

"I'm glad we won the prize money," Henry said. "But we still don't have enough to buy Grandfather's birthday present at the Greenfield Bookshop."

"We'll have enough money when we figure out who has been trying to ruin the fair," Benny said.

"We'll have enough left over to buy balloons and party hats, too. There's a $50 reward for solving the mystery," Violet said.

"*If* we can solve the mystery," Jessie said.

"It's still hard to believe all the things that have happened since we first saw that fair poster," Violet said.

"What we need to do now is figure out why anyone would want to ruin the fair contests," Henry said.

"Maybe they wanted the trophy and the money," Benny suggested.

"Or maybe someone wanted to get even with the people who were competing," Jessie said.

"Mrs. Stephens has been at every event and she's never won anything," Benny said.

"Susie has been at every event, too," Jessie pointed out.

"Also," Henry said, "Susie's pie and Mrs. Stephens's cake were the only ones not ruined today."

"It could just be a coincidence," Jessie said.

"Maybe," Henry said.

"We found the trophy and the prize money in Kristie's bag," Benny reminded everyone.

"Kristie does seem like the most likely suspect," Henry said.

"But Kristie looked very surprised when she found out the things were in her bag," Violet said.

"True," Jessie said, "but Kristie has been acting very strange lately."

"Kristie *has* been acting kind of strange," Violet agreed, "but I think it's because she didn't really want to enter the contest in the first place."

"What about the man in the baseball cap?" Benny said. "He always seems to be around when something has gone wrong."

"Yes," Violet said, "but he hasn't been entered in any of the contests."

"But he sure acts suspiciously," Jessie said.

"Maybe if we see him tomorrow we can follow him," Henry said.

"I can help you follow him," Benny offered. "I'll be very quiet so he won't know I'm around."

"This I'd like to see," Jessie said as she smiled at her noisy younger brother.

"I sure wish I knew who that girl was Kristie saw in the art tent," Violet said.

"When we see Kristie tomorrow maybe we can ask her again," Henry said.

"Speaking of tomorrow," Jessie said, "we'd better go to bed now. The livestock show starts early in the morning. And we've got a mystery to solve."

The next morning, as the children were getting ready to leave for the fair, the phone rang.

"Alden residence," Jessie said. She listened quietly for a moment, then she said, "Oh, I'm sorry to hear that, Courtney. Tell Michael I hope he feels better soon. I'll call you after the fair and tell you everything that happened."

"Is something wrong?" Violet asked.

"Michael isn't feeling well this morning,"

Jessie said. "Courtney says they won't be able to go to the fair with us today because she has to baby-sit Michael."

"That's too bad," Henry said. "We were all having so much fun."

"We sure were," Violet agreed. "I hope Michael feels well enough to come to Grandfather's birthday party tomorrow."

"Courtney said that she's going to make sure Michael stays in bed all day today," Jessie said. "He should feel better by tomorrow."

"I hope so," Benny said. "Why don't we make him a get-well card when we get home?"

"That's a wonderful idea, Benny," Violet said. "We can make a card for Grandfather's birthday, too."

"Well, we'd better hurry if we're going to get to the fair before it starts," Jessie said.

"And get back in time to buy Grandfather's birthday gift," Henry said.

The children ran as fast as they could to the fairgrounds. The livestock show was just starting when they arrived.

"I love the livestock show!" Benny said.

"I love this show, too," Violet said. "The animals are so beautiful."

"The parade is about to begin," Henry said.

"Ladies, gentlemen, boys, and girls," the announcer said. "Welcome to the Greenfield County Livestock Show! Now we will begin the animal promenade, after which the animals will be on display in the livestock tent. See if you can pick the winner of the Best of Show ribbon and the $25 cash prize! Good luck, everyone!"

The crowd began to cheer as the parade began. Children and adults marched into the arena with their animals beside them. Horses, sheep, goats, cows, and pigs, some with bright ribbons tied around their necks, walked alongside their owners. They mooed, baaed, and squealed noisily as they paraded around and around the ring.

"Look at that little horse," Benny said. "I could ride that one."

"That's a pony, Benny," Violet said.

"Look at all the pretty ribbons tied in its mane."

"It's beautiful," Jessie said. "And so well trained."

The pony obediently pranced beside its owner, a little girl who wore matching yellow ribbons in her hair. The judges made notes as each contestant passed. They smiled at the little girl and her pony when they stopped in front of their booth. The pony bowed to the judges.

"The judges liked that," Henry said as the contestants marched around the tent. "I'll bet the pony will win."

The judges talked together for a few moments and rose to make their announcement.

"The winner of the Greenfield County Livestock Show is Cindy Morgan and her pony, Dancer!"

"I knew they were going to win," Henry said. The little girl smiled as the judges presented her with the trophy and the prize money. She took the Best of Show ribbon and tied it to Dancer's mane. The crowd cheered and applauded.

The Boxcar Children walked down the bleachers and headed toward the exits with the rest of the crowd.

"Did you notice that nothing unusual happened during this contest?" Jessie said.

"What do you mean?" Henry asked.

"Well," Jessie continued. "In all the other events something went wrong. But this one went smoothly."

"Maybe it's because the person who is causing all the trouble at the fair didn't enter the livestock show," Violet said.

"I think you're right," Henry said.

"We'd better go over to the arts competition tent," Violet said. "I want to make sure nothing goes wrong during that event."

Suddenly Benny grabbed Violet's arm.

"Look over there," Benny said. "It's the man in the baseball cap."

The man in the baseball cap stood near the judges' booth. He held a pen and a notebook. From time to time, he looked suspiciously around the crowded tent. Then he wrote something down in his notebook.

"Now's our chance to follow him, Benny," Henry said.

"Good luck," Jessie said. "We'll be in the art tent. Meet us there as soon as you can."

"Okay," Benny said. The boys moved quickly through the crowd toward the man in the baseball cap. They were only a few feet from him when he turned to leave the tent.

"I hope they can keep up with him," Violet said.

"We'd better hurry," Jessie said. "The arts competition will be starting soon."

As the girls headed toward the art tent, Jessie spotted Susie Martinilli.

"Hi, Susie," Jessie called. "Wait for us."

"Hello," Susie said, smiling. "Are you going to the art tent?"

"Yes," Violet said. "Are you?"

"I am in just a minute," Susie said. "By the way, how did things go at the crafts exhibit yesterday?"

"It was pretty exciting there for a while," Jessie said. "Someone took the prize money, the trophy, and the blue ribbon."

"Really?" Susie said. "How awful! What happened?"

"It appears someone took the prizes while the judges were gone," Violet said. "Luckily, we found them in a bag behind the crafts tent."

"Goodness," Susie said. "There's been one problem after another at this fair."

"There sure has," Jessie agreed.

"Oh, Susie," Violet said. "There's a yellow stain on your pretty pink blouse."

"Oh, no," Susie said. She rubbed at the spot for a moment. "I was in such a hurry I didn't even notice it."

"It's still damp," Violet said. "That looks like Shimmery Yellow No. 7. Is it?"

"Why, yes," Susie said. "I just touched up my painting with it. I must have gotten some of it on my blouse."

"I've spilled that paint on my clothes before," Violet said. "All you have to do is rinse it out with water to remove the stain."

"Well, I don't have time to worry about it now," Susie said. "The art competition starts in a few minutes, and I've got something I need to do first. I'll see you later."

"Good-bye," Violet said as Susie hurried away.

"That's odd," Jessie said. "I thought the only colors in Susie's painting of the horse were browns and greens."

"Maybe she mixed blue with yellow to make green," Violet said. "But her painting looked finished to me."

"Let's take a look at it when we get inside," Jessie said.

The art tent was rapidly getting more and more crowded. The girls looked around for Henry and Benny.

"I guess they're still following that man in the baseball cap," Jessie said. "Maybe they'll be here later."

"Let's look at Susie's painting while we're waiting," Violet said.

The two girls carefully examined Susie's painting.

"This painting is perfectly dry," Violet said. "She didn't add any yellow paint to it at all."

"Why did she tell us she did?" Jessie said.

"I don't know," Violet said. "But I'm sure going to find out."

"Where is Kristie's painting?" Jessie said as she looked at the display. "It was on that easel over there yesterday."

"There's Mrs. Stephens," Violet said. "Let's ask her."

"Hello, Mrs. Stephens," Violet said as the woman approached them.

"Girls," Mrs. Stephens said worriedly. "Have either one of you seen Kristie?"

"No, we haven't seen her today," Violet said.

"What's wrong?" Jessie asked.

"Kristie sent me a note," Mrs. Stephens said. "It said that she didn't feel well and that she wanted me to meet her at the registration tent. But when I went to the tent she wasn't there and no one had seen her."

"Was her painting withdrawn from the competition?" Violet asked.

"Of course not," Mrs. Stephens said.

"Mrs. Stephens," Violet said. "Kristie's painting isn't here."

"Oh, no," Mrs. Stephens said as she stared at the empty easel. "Someone must have moved it while I was looking for Kristie. I have to find Kristie right away! The contest is getting ready to start."

"We'll help you look for her," Jessie said. "I'm sure she's not far away."

"She worked so hard on her painting," Mrs. Stephens said. "I don't know why she'd take it off the easel."

"Maybe she didn't," Jessie said. "May I see the note Kristie wrote to you?"

"Of course," Mrs. Stephens said. She looked puzzled but she handed the note to Jessie. Jessie slowly read the note. Then something caught her eye.

"Mrs. Stephens," Jessie said. "Is this Kristie's handwriting?"

"Why, no," Mrs. Stephens said as she read the note again. "It's not her handwriting! I was so upset when I got it that I didn't even notice."

"I'm going to ask the judges if they can delay the contest for a few moments," Jessie said. "Something's not right here." Jessie walked over to the contest table. She whispered softly to the judges for a moment. They nodded their heads.

"They'll give us ten minutes," Jessie said.

"We'll go with you to see if we can find Kristie," Violet said.

"Thank you very much, girls," Mrs. Stephens said.

Jessie and Violet followed Mrs. Stephens out of the art tent. Suddenly, Violet saw something sticking up out of a garbage can near the entrance. It sparkled in the sunlight.

"Look!" Violet said. She pulled the canvas out of the trash can. "It's Kristie's painting. There are yellow streaks all over it! It's ruined!"

"Oh, no!" cried Mrs. Stephens.

Violet touched the paint. It was still wet.

"We may be able to remove most of the paint streaks if we rinse it under cold water right away," Violet said.

"I'll take care of that," Jessie said. "Go with Mrs. Stephens and see if you can find Kristie. I'll clean this up and put it back on the easel at the art tent."

"Thank you," Mrs. Stephens said. "I appreciate your help."

"You're welcome," Jessie said. "I'm sure everything will be just fine."

"I hope so," Mrs. Stephens said nervously. "I certainly hope so."

Violet and Mrs. Stephens searched the fairgrounds for several minutes but there was no sign of Kristie.

"Do you think she might be waiting for you at your car?" Violet said. "Maybe someone gave her a phony note, too."

"That's a good idea," Mrs. Stephens said. "We've checked everywhere except the parking lot."

As they neared the parking lot, Violet saw Kristie.

"Kristie," Violet said as she ran toward her friend. "How are you feeling?"

"I'm just fine," Kristie said. She looked puzzled. "I was in the art tent when I got a note that said for me to meet my mother at the parking lot immediately."

"What?" Mrs. Stephens said. "I never sent you a note. I got a note a few minutes ago that said you were ill."

"I'm fine, Mother," Kristie said. "Someone must be playing some kind of awful joke on us."

"Do you still have that note, Kristie?" Violet asked.

"Yes," Kristie said. She pulled a slip of paper out of her pocket. Violet compared the two notes.

"These notes were written by the same person," Violet said. "Come on. Let's go back to the art tent."

"What happened to your painting, Kristie?" Violet asked, as they hurried back to the competition. "Someone painted yellow streaks all over it."

"It was on the display easel when I left the tent this morning," Kristie said. "I can't believe all this is happening. I never wanted to enter this contest in the first place."

"I'm sorry, dear," Mrs. Stephens said. "I never should have made you do it."

"That's all right, Mother," Kristie said. "The next time I paint something, it will be because I really want to."

"I think that's a good idea," Mrs. Stephens said as she hugged her daughter.

The contest had already begun by the time they returned to the tent. Jessie waved when she saw them. She had saved seats for them.

"I got most of that paint off," Jessie said to Kristie. "I put it back on the easel for you."

Kristie's painting still had a few streaks of yellow paint on it. The judges were examining it carefully.

"I hate to admit it," Kristie whispered to Violet. "But my painting looks even better! Those shiny yellow streaks look just like sunlight."

"You're right," Violet said. "It looks beautiful."

Violet pulled the notes out of her pocket and handed them to Jessie. "Someone sent these notes to Kristie and her mother," she whispered to her sister.

Jessie looked at both notes carefully. "I've seen this handwriting somewhere before. But I can't remember where."

Before Violet could ask her anything else, Kristie tapped her on the arm.

"The judges are getting ready to announce their decision," Kristie said.

"Good luck," Violet whispered.

"Good luck to you, too," Kristie whispered back.

"Ladies, gentlemen, boys, and girls," the judge said. "It is time to announce the winner of the Greenfield County Fair Art Competition."

Kristie and Violet held hands tightly.

"The winner is contestant Miss Susie Martinilli!"

Susie stepped forward to receive the trophy and prize money.

"That's the girl that was in the tent the day my book bag was taken!" Kristie said.

Before the judge could hand Susie the prize money and the trophy, Jessie stood up.

"Just a minute, please," Jessie said. "I think that there has been a violation of the rules."

"I think so, too," said another voice. Jessie looked around. It was the man in the baseball cap. Henry and Benny were standing next to him.

CHAPTER 9

The Mystery Is Solved

The judge asked the crowd to please be patient for ten minutes while the rules violation was examined. Then he asked the Alden children, Susie, Mrs. Stephens, Kristie, and the man in the baseball cap to follow him. Everyone crowded inside the judge's small office.

"Now," the judge said after he closed the door. "What's going on here?"

Jessie gave the notes to the judge. He laid the notes side by side on a small table.

"These are notes which were given to Mrs.

Stephens and her daughter, Kristie," Jessie said. "I think that whoever wrote these notes did it so that Kristie and her mother would be away from the tent when Kristie's painting was removed and damaged. The handwriting on the notes is the same."

"Who do you think did this?" the judge asked.

"I think Susie wrote those notes," Jessie said.

"That's ridiculous," Susie cried, "you can't prove anything."

"When you borrowed my pen at registration tent, I noticed that you dot your i's with little hearts," Jessie said.

"Lots of people sign their names like that," Susie said. "That doesn't mean anything."

"How did you get that yellow paint on your blouse, Susie?" Violet asked. "The yellow paint that made the stain on your blouse is made to reflect the light. None of the paint on your artwork does that."

"Also, you asked me how the necklace was held together. You knew that cutting the wire would ruin our necklace," Jessie said.

"And what about Kristie's book bag?" Henry said. "Did you take it to make it look like Kristie was the one who was causing all the trouble at the fair?"

"You don't know what you're talking about," Susie said. She looked scared.

"I think they do," the man with the baseball cap said. "Judge, I'm Steven Pearson. The fair officials hired me to investigate the problems which have been happening since the fair was announced."

"So that's why we kept seeing you everywhere," Jessie said.

"But why were you always hurrying away when something bad happened?" Violet asked.

"I didn't want anyone to notice me," Mr. Pearson answered. "But you children were too clever for me."

"When we finally got a chance to talk with Mr. Pearson, he told us that he was curious about the same things we are," Henry said.

"At first we were following him," Benny chimed in. "Now we're working together."

"You children have done most of my job

for me," Mr. Pearson said. "Susie, I think you have a lot of explaining to do."

"I don't know why I've been so mean," Susie said. "My family and I are moving away in a few weeks, and I felt like this was my last chance to win a trophy. I'm really sorry for the way I've ruined things for everyone. I know I don't deserve to win anything." Then she burst into tears.

"Susie, we decided on the first day of the contest that your artwork was one of the best," the judge said. "You could have won a trophy this year if only you had competed honestly."

"I'm sorry," Susie said sadly, tears still streaming down her cheeks. "I really am."

"The Alden children will be receiving a $50 reward for solving this mystery," the judge said. "Thank you."

"You're welcome," Henry said.

"We're glad we were able to help," Jessie said.

"Thank you, children, for making my job much easier," Mr. Pearson said, smiling.

"But what about the posters?" Benny

asked. "Who tore up all the posters?"

"I'm afraid I did that too," Susie replied. "I thought if there weren't as many entries this year, I'd have a better chance of winning."

"I'm sure the contest officials would like to speak with you, Susie," Mr. Pearson said. "Please come with me."

Susie followed Mr. Pearson out of the office.

"I didn't want to say anything," Kristie said. "But I saw Susie ruining the pies the first day of the fair."

"So that's why you were so upset that day," Violet said.

"Why didn't you tell anyone?" Henry asked.

"I was going to," Kristie said, "but then you found those prizes in my book bag. I didn't think anyone would believe me if I told them what I'd seen in the pie tent."

"That's probably why Susie put the prizes in your book bag in the first place," Jessie said. "She must have known that you'd seen her ruining the pies. I'll bet she was hoping everyone would think you were the guilty one."

"I guess so," Kristie said. "I'm glad this whole thing is finally over."

"Not yet," the judge said. "Your beautiful painting of a sunset received the second largest number of votes. You are now the winner!"

"Congratulations, Kristie," Violet said.

"Thank you," Kristie said.

"Let's make the announcement to the crowd," the judge said, smiling. "They've waited long enough to meet the real winner of the Greenfield County Fair Art Competition!"

After the fair was over, the Boxcar Children went shopping. Their first stop was the Greenfield Bookshop.

"Hello there! Nice to see you again," Mr. Owens said when the children entered the shop.

"Hello, Mr. Owens," Jessie said. "We're back to buy that book for our grandfather."

"I have it right here," Mr. Owens said. He handed the beautiful book to Jessie. "I'm glad you were able to earn enough money to buy it."

"So are we," Henry said as he paid for the book.

"Grandfather will be so surprised," Benny said.

"He sure will," Violet said. "Thank you for holding it for us, Mr. Owens."

"It was my pleasure," Mr. Owens said.

"Let's go buy some balloons and party hats," Henry said. "Good-bye, Mr. Owens."

"Good-bye, children," the shopkeeper said. "Have fun."

The children bought everything they needed for the party.

CHAPTER 10

The Surprise

The next morning, Jessie got up early to wrap Grandfather's birthday present. Violet made a special birthday card for their grandfather and a get-well card for Michael. Benny blew up balloons. And Henry hung beautifully colored crepe paper streamers all over the dining room. By lunchtime, everything was finished.

"The place looks lovely, children," Mrs. McGregor said as she placed the birthday cake in the center of the table.

"Grandfather should be home soon," Violet said. "Everyone needs to sign his card before he arrives."

"I can't wait to see his face when he opens our present," Jessie said. "He's going to be so surprised."

The children heard the key turning in the lock.

"Hide everyone!" Jessie said. "Grandfather's home."

Grandfather came into the dining room.

"Surprise! Surprise!" the children shouted. "Happy Birthday, Grandfather."

"My, my, my," Grandfather said. "I *am* surprised. What lovely decorations."

"I blew up all the balloons," Benny said.

"Good job, Benny," Grandfather said. "Now I have a surprise for you!"

Michael and Courtney ran into the room.

"Michael! Courtney!" the children shouted.

"We're so glad you could come to the party," Jessie said.

"So are we," Courtney said. "We got here the same time your Grandfather did."

"We made a get-well card for Michael,"

Violet said. She handed the brightly decorated card to the little boy.

"Thank you!" Michael said.

"How are you feeling, Michael?" Henry asked.

"I'd feel even better if I had some birthday cake," Michael said.

Everyone laughed. Mrs. McGregor lit the candles on the cake and everyone sang Happy Birthday to Mr. Alden. He cut slices of the cake and passed them around to everyone. Then he opened his card.

"What a lovely card!" Grandfather said. Then he carefully unwrapped the paper and saw the beautiful book. *"The History of Greenfield,"* Grandfather said. "This is a very special book, and expensive, too. You children must have worked very hard to buy it."

The Aldens all smiled at each other.

"I've been wanting this book for a long time," Grandfather said. "How did you know?"

"Oh, that mystery was easy to solve," Benny said as he started on his second piece of birthday cake.

GERTRUDE CHANDLER WARNER discovered when she was teaching that many readers who like an exciting story could find no books that were both easy and fun to read. She decided to try to meet this need, and her first book, *The Boxcar Children*, quickly proved she had succeeded.

Miss Warner drew on her own experiences to write the mystery. As a child she spent hours watching trains go by on the tracks opposite her family home. She often dreamed about what it would be like to set up housekeeping in a caboose or freight car — the situation the Alden children find themselves in.

When Miss Warner received requests for more adventures involving Henry, Jessie, Violet, and Benny Alden, she began additional stories. In each, she chose a special setting and introduced unusual or eccentric characters who liked the unpredictable.

While the mystery element is central to each of Miss Warner's books, she never thought of them as strictly juvenile mysteries. She liked to stress the Aldens' independence and resourcefulness and their solid New England devotion to using up and making do. The Aldens go about most of their adventures with as little adult supervision as possible — something else that delights young readers.

Miss Warner lived in Putnam, Connecticut, until her death in 1979. During her lifetime, she received hundreds of letters from girls and boys telling her how much they liked her books.

The Fun Starts Here!

There's nothing quite like a county fair. That's where you'll find fun games, cool crafts, and yummy food. In fact, there's only one other place where you'll find all of those. Can you guess where that might be? Yep, you guessed it — right here in these activity pages.

The Puzzle Competition

Step right up and try your luck.
Okay, okay, maybe it takes a little more than luck to solve these puzzles. It takes brain power. But that's okay — we know you're a winner in that department!

A Wheel-y Fun Time!

The Boxcar Children just love fairs. Henry likes going on fast rides. Violet enjoys looking at the crafts. Jessie, who adores animals, can't wait for the livestock competitions. Do you know what Benny loves best? Go around the wheel. Write every other letter in the spaces below, and you will see.

Benny likes __ __ __   __ __ __ __ __

Where To? Word Search

Now that they've finally arrived at the fair, the Boxcar Children don't know where to go first. This word search is filled with things to do and see at a county fair. Can you find them all? The words go up, down, sideways, backwards, and diagonally.

Look for: **CANDY APPLES, FERRIS WHEEL, BUMPER CAR, PIGS, COWS, PIES, RIBBONS, GAMES, FRIENDS, BANDS, SHOWS, PRIZES, LEMONADE, HOT DOGS, TENTS**

```
F C O W S L Z S D N A B G
E V A H B C D N P A B U A
R E S N O B B I R Z M M M
R D A A D R Z D I S S P E
I A V S E Y A V Z H T E S
S N T D C L A W E O N R R
W O E N I J P P S W E C O
H M N E L K I L P S T A A
E E P I G G M L I L U R W
E L V R S W A X H S E I P
L M C F D H O T D O G S K
```

Flowery Fun

Violet is a wonderful artist. Her favorite things to paint are flowers. And not just violets, either. Her paintings are filled with roses, pansies, lilies, and tulips, too.

You can color a flowery picture. Add up the numbers in each section. Then, use your crayons and follow the code.

Color the sections that add up to 5, pink.
Color the sections that add up to 12, green.
Color the sections that add up to 9, yellow.
Color the sections that add up to 14, red.
Color the sections that add up to 11, purple.
Color the sections that add up to 20, white.

This Little Piggy

It is time to judge the livestock competition. Which pig will win the contest? Find the one that's different.

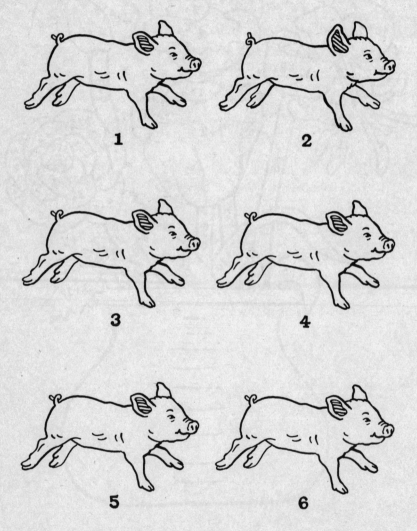

Balloon-acy!

Oh, no! The balloon man let go of his balloons. Now they are flying all over. Can you find all of his balloons? When you do, color three of them yellow, two of them blue, one of them black, five of them red, and four of them green. How many balloons did you find?

We Love a Parade!

On opening day at the county fair, there is always a big parade! Here's a marching song you can sing and march in time to.

The Bear Went Over the Mountain

The bear went over the mountain.
The bear went over the mountain.
The bear went over the mountain,
and what do you think he saw?

He saw another mountain.
He saw another mountain.
He saw another mountain,
and what do you think he did?

He climbed that other mountain.
He climbed that other mountain.
He climbed that other mountain,
and what do you think he saw?

He saw another mountain.
He saw another mountain.
He saw another mountain,
and what do you think he did?

(Go back to the beginning of the song)

Let's Hear It For The Band!

Now that you've practiced marching, it's time to strike up the band. Here are some simple instruments to make.

Terrific Tambourine!

You will need: Hard candies, small paper plates, aluminum foil, ribbons, scissors, and a stapler.
Here's what you do: Put the candies on top of a paper plate. Cover the candies with the second paper plate. This will make a sort of plate and candy sandwich. Staple the plates together. Go all around the circle. Make sure the staples are really close together so the candies do not fall out.

Cut 7 small (three inches around) circles of aluminum foil. Place the aluminum circles around the rim of the top plate. Leave a small space without a circle. Staple the circles through both plates.

Cut several lengths of different colored ribbons. Gather them together, and staple them to the small space you left between the circles.

Now shake, shake, shake your tambourine!

Rum Tum Tum Drum

You will need: A round cardboard salt or oatmeal container, masking tape, construction paper, crayons or markers.

Here's what you do: Cut the construction paper large enough to wrap around the container. Decorate the paper with a crayon or marker. Tape your decorated paper to the container. Bang your drum to the beat.

The Crafts Corner!

At a county fair, crafts are everywhere! The great thing about crafts is that you can have just as good a time making them as you do using them. Here are some crafty things you can put together. You make them using things from around the house — the same way the Alden children made things when they lived inside their Boxcar.

Bean Beads

Jessie and Courtney used sparkling African beads to make their jewelry. You don't have to travel all the way to Africa to make beautiful beaded necklaces. You only have to travel as far as your kitchen!

You will need: dried kidney, lima, pinto, and lentil beans, glue, 12 inches of strong thread, a kitchen knife, clear nail polish, and a grown-up.

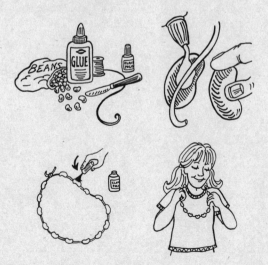

Here's what you do: Ask the grown-up to cut the beans in half, the long way. Put a spot of glue about 2 inches from the end of the thread. Slip half a bean under the glue-covered spot of thread. Slip the other half on top of the thread. Squeeze the halves of the bean together. Wipe off any excess glue. Glue more beans along the thread the same way until you have used as many beans and covered as much of the thread as you like. Tie the ends of the thread together in a knot. Once the glue is dry, ask your favorite grown-up to help you coat the beans in clear nail polish. Allow the polish to dry before you try on your creation.

Whirly Copters!

These hilarious helicopters are big hits — at the county fair or anywhere!

You will need: a strip of paper 1.5 inches × 10 inches, 1 paper clip

Here's what you do: Fold your strip of paper in half lengthwise. Follow the pictures to see how to fold the rest of your paper. Then place the paper clip at the bottom part of your copter. Throw it high in the air and watch it whirl!

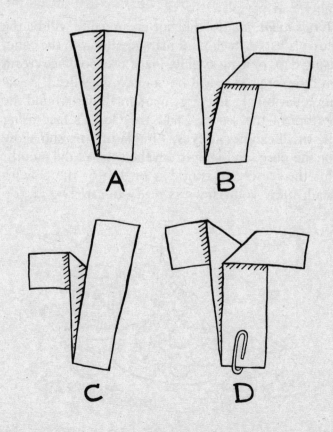

A   B

C   D

The Snack Bar!

It's time for something to eat. Why not try one of these sweet treats? Benny personally recommends each and every one of them!

The Clowning Around Ice Cream Cone

You will need: ice cream (any flavor you like), an ice cream scoop, an ice cream cone, miniature and regular marshmallows, small candies, gel icing (in a tube), a paper plate

Here's what you do: The ice cream cone will be the clown's hat. Attach mini marshmallows to the cone, using dabs of icing as glue. Place a scoop of ice cream on the plate. This will be your clown's head. Make his collar by placing large marshmallows around the bottom of the scoop. Make the clown's face using the small candies as eyes, a miniature marshmallow for the nose, and icing from the tube as the mouth. Put the ice cream cone hat on top of the clown's head. Now your clown is ready to eat! Dig in!

Benny's Blue Ribbon Pie Recipe!

You will need: 1 pint sherbet (any flavor you like), 1 8 oz. tub of whipped topping, 1 ready-made pie crust, 9 chocolate sandwich cookies chopped, mixing bowl, spoon

Here's what you do: Place the sherbet in the bowl and stir until smooth. Stir in ½ the whipped topping until it is well blended with the sherbet. Spoon the sherbet topping mixture into the pie crust. Sprinkle the chopped cookies on top of the mixture. Cover the chopped cookies with the rest of the whipped topping.

Freeze your pie for four hours. Let it stand at room temperature for 10 minutes before serving.

Answers

A Wheel-y Fun Time
Benny likes THE FOOD.

Where To? Word Search

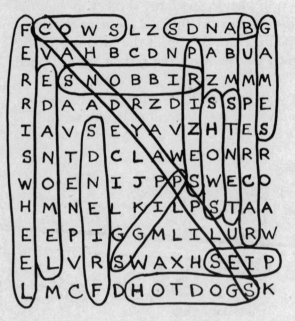

This Little Piggy
Number two is the winner.

Balloon-acy
There are 15 balloons.